Chapter One

Miss Minkin the tabby cat lived at Ghyllside Farm. Her best friend was a Hob who lived under the hearthstone.

He came out in the evenings
when the farm family had all gone
to bed, and he and Miss Minkin
shared a bowl of cream, and spent
the night very happily telling tales,
singing old songs, and sometimes
dancing on the hearth.

The Hob and Miss Minkin

The Naming Song

Sandra Ann Horn

Illustrated by Amanda Harvey

Hodder
Children's
Books

a division of Hodder Headline plc

For the next generation of Ghyllside Farm folk,
my brothers Glyn and Frank,
and sisters-in-law Carol and Susan,
with love

Text Copyright © 1999 Sandra Ann Horn
Illustrations Copyright ©1999 Amanda Harvey

First published in Great Britain in 1999
by Hodder Children's Books

The right of Sandra Ann Horn and Amanda Harvey to be identified as the
Author and Illustrator of the Work has been asserted by them in accordance
with the Copyright, Designs and Patents Act 1988.

10   9   8   7   6   5   4   3   2   1

A Catalogue record for this book is available from the British Library

ISBN 0340 72277 0
Printed and bound in Great Britain by
Guernsey Press, Channel Islands

Hodder Children's Books
A Division of Hodder Headline plc
338 Euston Road
London NW1 3BH

Hob played the fiddle, and Miss Minkin had a very fine soprano voice.

Miss Minkin was very fussy about her appearance. She washed and smoothed her beautiful fur several times a day. "I like to be clean," said Miss Minkin.

Jenny the farmer's wife liked
to be clean too. She kept the house
neat and tidy all year round, but
every spring she went cleaning mad.

She tidied, dusted, scrubbed and
polished the house from attics to
cellars and there was nothing anybody
could do about it. It was most
upsetting to Miss Minkin's nerves.

Chapter Two

One spring morning, Miss Minkin was dozing on the hearth when Jenny flew downstairs with her arms full of dusters, mops and polishing cloths. Hob had vanished with the first light of dawn.

He was in his secret place
deep under the hearthstone, where
he had lived for hundreds of years.
Nobody knew he was there except
Miss Minkin, and she would not tell.

Miss Minkin was waiting for
Jenny to bring her breakfast, but no
breakfast came. When she meowed
very loudly to remind Jenny about
it, Jenny only said, "I'm too busy
spring cleaning to think about
anything else. Why don't you fend
for yourself? Go and catch something."

Miss Minkin could hardly believe her ears. She did not want to go and catch something.

She wanted her dish of nice white fish with all the bones taken out, and she sat up very straight in the middle of the kitchen with her back to Jenny and thrashed her tail from side to side until Jenny said, "Oh all right then – but you can have it outside so you're not under my feet."

"Under her feet! How very rude," said Miss Minkin under her breath. She would like to have stalked off with her tail in the air and not come back until Jenny thought she was lost forever and would be sorry, but she was too hungry. She ate all the fish first and *then* stalked off.

Chapter Three

In the evening, when the house was quiet, Miss Minkin slipped back through the cat flap into the kitchen, and hoped that Hob would soon appear from under the hearthstone.

She could tell him what a dreadful day she'd had, and how nobody had nice manners any more.

But what was this? Miss Minkin stopped and stared. The fire was out! The hearth was swept clean, and in the grate was a heap of crinkly red paper instead of warm glowing coal.

"This," said Miss Minkin, "is the giddy limit."

"What is?" said Hob, appearing from the shadows. "I see the fire-irons have been polished. Shine up nice, don't they? And the fire's been let out. It must be spring. I thought there was something in the air."

"Old mother mouse has built a nest under the wash-house floor, and she's got a nice little brood in there – must be seven or eight mousekins."

Miss Minkin pricked up her ears. "Oh really?" she said, licking her lips and looking thoughtful.

Hob got out his pipe. "That's a good dish of cream," he said.

Jenny always left a dish of cream for Miss Minkin, and she shared it with Hob, turn by turn. The dish was brimful.

"I expect it's Jenny's way of saying sorry for being so unkind," said Miss Minkin, "and I forgive her, but the hearthstone is cold with the fire out and I'm not very comfortable. I do not like spring, it is too much of a disturbance."

Hob scratched his head.
"We could sit in the fireplace, on
the crinkly paper," he suggested,
"it might be quite cosy. What do
you think, my dear? I'll bring the
cream."

19

Miss Minkin said she would try it, although it wasn't what she was used to.

She climbed into the fireplace and kneaded the paper with her paws into a soft red nest. Hob said it was better than a cushion.

He looked up the chimney.
"Look up yonder," he said.
There above them was
a sickle moon and a
single bright star.

"Beautiful,"
purred Miss Minkin,
"shall we serenade
it, my dear?"

Hob got
out his fiddle,
Miss Minkin
cleared her throat, and
they sang a couple of verses of
'O Silver Moon' before getting down
to the cream.

Miss Minkin said it was a happy
ending to a very trying day.

Chapter Four

Next morning, Jenny was still cleaning and turning out cupboards, but she did remember Miss Minkin's breakfast.

After she had finished, Miss Minkin curled up in the airing cupboard among the blankets for a morning nap, but she was soon turned out again by Jenny.

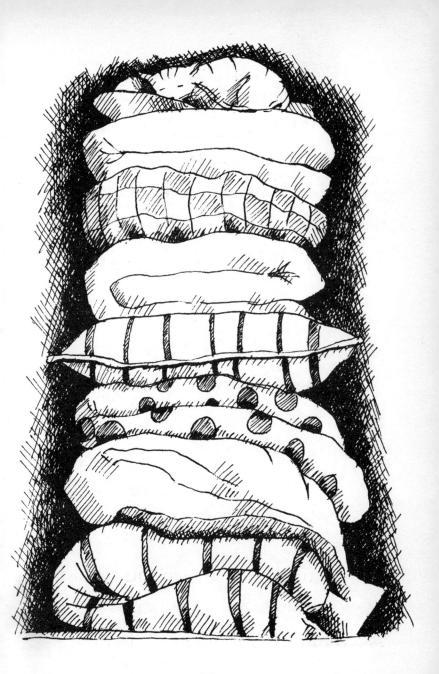

23

"Sheer madness!" muttered Miss Minkin, "Taking everything out and putting it back again. She should see the vet and get something for her nerves, in my opinion."

Unfortunately, no one was listening.

Miss Minkin left the racketty house and went to the barn, thinking she would have a snooze in the hay, but what did she see? Her own special hole in the bottom of the door was covered up with a piece of wood.

She could hear some very interesting noises from inside the barn; "cheep! cheep! cheep!"

She pushed at the wood with her paw.

"Oi!" shouted the farmer, "You keep away from there, pussy! There's newly-hatched chicks in there."

Miss Minkin put her head on one side as if to say, "Oh, please – I only want to play Chase and Pounce with them."

"SCAT!!" said the farmer, very loud and cross. Miss Minkin left, hurriedly.

She spent the day in the woodpile, which was rather damp and cobwebby.

Chapter Five

That evening, when the house was quiet and they thought everyone had gone to bed, Hob and Miss Minkin met on the hearth as usual.

There was still no fire, but Miss Minkin said she was getting used to it.

Hob was in a dancing mood,
so they danced a stately gavotte on
the hearthstone before climbing into
the fireplace with the cream dish.

They were almost at the last drop of
cream when there was a scuffling
noise above them, and a lump of
soot fell into the dish.

Miss Minkin declared she could not touch another morsel now, but Hob didn't mind a bit of honest dirt, so he scraped the bowl out.

Then there was a scratching noise, and more soot. Hob looked up the chimney. Instead of a moon in a dark blue sky, he saw a mass of twigs.

"Oh ho!" he said, "bird's nest!"

Miss Minkin pricked up her ears. "How lovely!" she said. "The moon is all very pretty, but it cannot compare with a nest full of dear little baby birds – and so convenient, too."

Hob looked gloomy. "That's all very well my dear," he said, "but we won't be sitting here in comfort any more. All sorts of rubbish will fall on us, and the chimney will be blocked, so when they come to light the fire again there'll be nothing but soot and smoke, and maybe the chimney afire."

Miss Minkin was about to say
that Hob was making a fuss about
nothing, when a very large lump of
soot fell on her left front paw, and
made her beautiful fur all black.
She looked up.
A rotten dusty
twig came
clattering down
and hit her
right on
her pink
nose.

Miss Minkin sneezed and said
"Yow!" She bared her teeth and
glared up the chimney.

The mother bird was looking down just then, and saw a pair of fierce green eyes and two rows of sharp teeth below, which she didn't like much at all.

"Bert, we'll have to move," she called to her husband. "I don't like it here. I want a nest in a tree like everybody else."

Her husband, who had been flying backwards and forwards with twigs all day until he was giddy, said, "Nonsense! You'll soon get used to it, and it's a very smart address."

Miss Minkin frowned. She had changed her mind about the bird's nest.

"Bother! They are going to stay," she said, "and we'll have to sit on the cold hearth or be showered with nasty rubbish every night."

Hob said nothing. He winked at Miss Minkin, then got out his pipe and lit it. He huffed and puffed, then began to blow smoke rings, one after the other. The smoke rings drifted up the chimney until they reached the nest.

The mother bird gave an angry squawk, then a cough.

"Fire!" she shouted. "You and your smart address, Bert Bird! We'll all be choked with smoke and fried to a crisp!"

"Oh, all right then!" said her husband. "We'll move. How was I to know they'd light the fire at this time of year? Come on, we'll spend the night in the barn and tomorrow we'll find another place."

"In a TREE this time," said his wife, and they flew off together, quarrelling as they went.

"Oh, well done, my dear," said
Miss Minkin.

"It was nothing," said Hob.
Then he waved his pipe three times
round and said "Begone!" up the
chimney, and the twigs hopped off
the chimney-pot and rolled down
into the gutter.

"Lovely view of the moon,"
said Miss Minkin.

Chapter Six

They settled down on the crinkly paper, and Miss Minkin began to wash the soot off her paw while Hob played a soft lilting tune on his fiddle. "Peace at last," purred Miss Minkin.

When the tune had ended and the kitchen fell quiet, Miss Minkin thought she would have a nice little wash. Halfway through, she stopped quite suddenly with one paw in the air, and swivelled her ears.

"What's that?" she said, "there's someone out in the yard. I thought they were all a-bed."

Hob swivelled his ears too.
"It's coming from the stable," he
said. "Something must be wrong out
there. Come on."

They slipped out of the cat flap.
The stable was across the yard, and
although it was dark the door was
open a little way, and a shaft of yellow
light lay over the ground like a path.

"Wait!" hissed Miss Minkin, "Someone's there. They might see you."

"Not a chance!" said Hob, "don't you worry."

Hob and Miss Minkin followed the bright path across the cobbles, and crept quietly in to the stable.

They stood in the shadows by the wall. Nobody saw them, and nobody heard. Jenny and her husband were trying to soothe a fretful mare, who was lying on the straw.

"She's having a foal," whispered Miss Minkin, "at teatime Jenny said she was taking her time about it."

By and by they saw a leggy new chestnut foal being born.

Jenny said, "She'll be all right now. It's been a long labour and she's worn out."

"Me too," said her husband, yawning, "Let's get some sleep."

Chapter Seven

Hob and Miss Minkin drew back deeper into the shadows.

Hob tugged his beard three times, and although Jenny and her husband passed by within an inch, they saw nothing but two withered turnips in the hay.

Then the two withered turnips
shook themselves, and anyone could
see that they were really a tabby cat
and a hob. They came out of the
shadows and crept up to the stall.

The mare was deep asleep, and
the little foal by her side was still
and silent. His eyes were open, but
he was not looking at anything.

"I don't like the look of him," said Hob. He walked up to the foal and said, "Hello little fellow!"

The foal did not move.

Hob waved his hand close to the foal's eyes.

He did not blink or stir.

"Whatever is the matter with him?" said Miss Minkin.

Hob scratched his head.

"I think he hasn't been sung his naming song, so he can't start being a horse yet," he said, "his mother must have fallen asleep before she could sing it. Let's try to wake her up."

48

Hob and Miss Minkin did their best. They patted the mare's face and said, "Hello!" very loud. They shouted and sang in her ear. She was far too tired to wake up.

"Nothing else for it," said Hob, "WE'LL have to horse him, or he won't know who he is."

"Mother cats name their kittens too," said Miss Minkin, "shall I sing their special song to him? It's about beautiful green eyes and sleek fur, sharp teeth and claws, pink tongues lapping milk, mousing and bird-catching ..."

"I don't think that would do at all, I'm afraid, my dear," said Hob, "I'll have to try and remember the horse song. My second cousin Fergal sang it to me once, but it was a long time ago and in Erse, of course. Hmm."

Hob paced round in the straw muttering to himself, but every time he thought he had remembered a bit of the song, there was a noise and it muddled him up. A bat scrabbled in the eaves, a mouse squeaked, a rat rustled in the straw, a moth blundered round the lamp.

"This is hopeless," he said.

Miss Minkin said she would fix it. She crouched like a tiger at the entrance to the stall and glared round the stable with her big green eyes. Then she began to growl, very low but very fierce.

All the scurrying creatures in the stable stood still for a second, and then dived for holes and burrows and perches and kept perfectly quiet until morning.

"Thank you my dear," said Hob, and then he began to pace and mutter once more. Finally, he said, "I think I've got it."

Hob walked up close to the little foal's ear, cleared his throat, and sang the horse-naming song. It had a strange-sounding tune like nothing Miss Minkin had ever heard before.

It began with the shadow-black horses who pull the silver chariot of the moon across the sky, and as Hob sang the stable seemed to fill with the winds of sleep, and stars thrown off by sparking hooves.

Miss Minkin saw the little horse's left ear twitch.

Then Hob sang about the golden steeds of the sun, scattering light from their streaming manes as they fly from the farthest east to the uttermost west.

The little horse twitched his right ear.

Miss Minkin held her breath.

The song went on to tell of
the foam-white storm horses of
the sea, with lightning in their eyes
and thunder in their galloping.

The little horse twitched both
his ears. "Oh bravo!" murmured
Miss Minkin.

Hob was nearly at full pitch
now, singing about carousel horses
with golden bridles and scarlet
manes, hobby horses with bells
on their bridles, and rocking horses
galloping across the floor to a
magical land far away.

The little horse lifted his head.

Miss Minkin sighed.

"Last of all and best of all,"
sang Hob "are the horses of earth; the
sure-footed children of the South Wind.
Once upon a day the wind caught up
handfuls of earth from all places and
all seasons, and he breathed on them.
He breathed on the black frosts
and white snows of winter,
the cloud-dappled ground of spring,
the gold of ripe summer wheat and
the silky autumn brown of chestnuts."

Miss Minkin could smell sweet meadow-grass as the song went on, and hear hooves and swishing tails under a wide sky.

The song ended with: "The South Wind breathed beauty and strength, speed and gentleness into them, and he named them Horse. You are a horse! Wake up and be!"

The little horse blinked, as if he could see something at last. He made a soft whinnying sound.

All at once his mother woke up, although it was only a very small whinny, and she snuggled close to him and whinnied back.

Miss Minkin wiped a tear from her eye. Hob and the mare looked at each other.

"It's all right," said Hob, "he's horsed." The mare nodded her head.

"Come on," said Hob to Miss Minkin, "let's be getting home-along, there's nothing more for us to do here."

They stepped through the stable door as the first light of a new spring day was silvering the Downs and the birds were waking up, and they stopped for a moment to breathe the morning air.

"Primroses will soon be opening on the ghyll bank," said Hob.

"Yes," said Miss Minkin, "it's a lovely time of year."

Then they slipped in through the cat flap as quietly as shadows.